THE SHIPWRECKED HOUSE

Claire Trévien was born in Brittany. Her pamphlet *Low-Tide Lottery* was published by Salt in 2011. She is the editor of Sabotage Reviews and the co-organiser of Penning Perfumes, a creative collaboration between poets and perfumers.

The Shipwrecked House

Claire Trévien

Penned in the Margins
LONDON

PUBLISHED BY PENNED IN THE MARGINS
Toynbee Studios, 28 Commercial Street, London E1 6AB
www.pennedinthemargins.co.uk

First published 2013

Printed in the United Kingdom by Bell & Bain Ltd.

ISBN
978-1-908058-11-9

Contents

Acknowledgements

Thank you to the following magazines, websites and anthologies in which versions of these poems have previously appeared: *Best British Poetry 2012, Birdbook 2, Clinic, Coin Opera 2, Dove Release: New Flights and Voices, Epicentre, Fuselit, The Great British Bard-Off, Ink, Sweat and Tears, Lung Jazz, Poetry Cornwall, Pomegranate, Under the Radar, The Warwick Review.*

Six poems originally appeared in my pamphlet *Low-Tide Lottery* (Salt Publishing, 2011): 'Entrepreneurs', 'Belleville', 'Novella', 'Rusty Sea', 'Beg an Dorchenn', 'Sing Bird'. The poem 'Métro' originally appeared in my e-chapbook *Patterns of Decay* (Silkworms Ink, 2011).

Special cheers to Tom Chivers, Lucy Ayrton, Katy Evans-Bush, Paul Davidson, Tim Wells, Claudia Haberberg, Emily Hasler, Lindsey Holland, Amy Key, Sophie Mayer, Ariane Samson-Divisa, Tori Truslow and Helen Weldon. Thank you to my family, especially Charlotte Coatalen Lambert for the cover art.

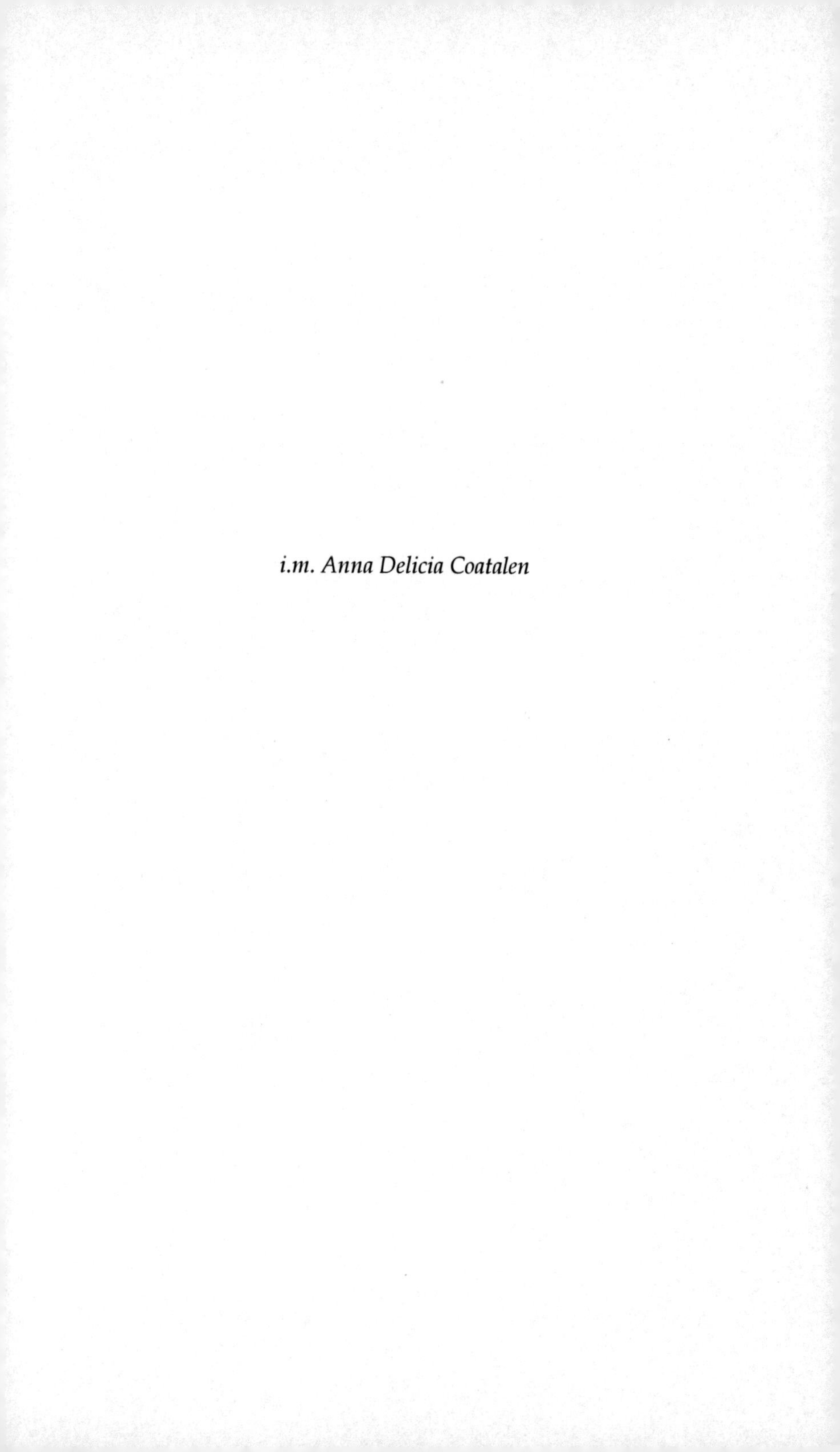

i.m. Anna Delicia Coatalen

The Shipwrecked House

Origin Story

They were to place seaweed in my cot
so that I'd grow with nets for hands
to better haul mica-strewn salmon.
Mistletoe-of-the-sea raised on the back
of crabs, collected at midnight for luck.

Instead, they brought me heather's bells
dangled noiselessly to taunt the crush
of my potato fists. They sewed its scales
into my skin, hushed my cries, taught
me that it grows where others cannot.

The Shipwrecked House I

The ceiling is tugged by the moon
it expands above us, an opaque dome
through which we guess the stars.

Other ships will be built from these rooms,
other seas and currents eroded by a figurehead.

Walls tremble violet-blue, weave the song
of seagulls into their granite veins.
An empty wine glass fills with cowries.

My mother twists her ring like a weathervane,
east to west; still the sun refuses to set.

Cowries are claimed from the sand;
fingers sniffle through broken claws.

We hinge the stones in pools to watch life
dart out and hide beneath other shelters.

The glass fills but is still half empty.
Ironed darned sheets cover old mattresses that spill
over the frames of beds.

And Cesária Évora sings of homesickness.

Wreck

After George Gunn

no Atlantis this forest of debris
twigs dulled by the sanding of stream
trunks edited by the tenuous

ships have been misplaced in its filing system
traces of light fade fast
smells are swallows too fast to track

opaque but not peaceful
the skittering of memories punctures
and steals another layer of paint

or another thread from the curtain

Whales

Whales lived under our house,
making the hinges rock, splitting cups and cheeks.

Stray socks melted in their comb-mouths
their fins sliced through conversations,
we found bones in our cups of tea.

Most of the time they just wanted to play
bounced against bookshelves, snorted leaks,
threw bodies across the room.

No one believed me of course,
the carpet looked too smooth to hide a mammal.

At night, I'd listen to their song
beat through the floorboards
like slashes of headlights.

For days they'd circle the house
take a dive into the cellar, press the doorbell
and run, I'd sometimes forget then trip
over the carcass of one beached
in the gutter.

Entrepreneurs

Entrepreneurs, we'd go hunting: small pigs,
oysters, whiskered fish, shells broken twice, thrice,
or more, smooth rocks, rough stones, papers and pegs,
then we'd open our restaurant: fresh turf

for entry, grained house water *à la carte,*
crabs that have *sautéed* on home-grown seaweed
for your main – served with *papier mâché* tart,
the pudding crawled away, but we have seeds

if you wish. To think we'd met knee deep in
the sea, both wanting that vinyl record,
your house was closest – so I let you win.
We chased all day and tripped till dusk with swords,

what a pair! Yet now, the food has dried or
left and the customers are in their beds.

The Shipwrecked House II

After Frank O'Hara

When waves were far enough away
and the pumpkin seeds still as amber
in the treasure chest, the calls tumblingly
came to crook the paintings, writings, all.

Now your voice falls like a coin to the ocean's floor
and the house is dragged apart by the fractures
of your smiles – the thought of its absence echoes
unbelievably – our breath opens like a stiff drawer.

You are everywhere and nowhere, you are
the unfinished cup of tea and its straw,
dipped like a paintbrush. I want to keep
the yoghurts that went out of date yesterday.

La Frégate

For Claude

His table was an island from which his words,
replenished ships, departed and never returned.

His seat is sat on by others now, their sticky elbows rub
the paper, transfer the words – ink that stains briefly, then goes.

Journeys of Evaporation

For Antony Gormley

The sand has risen and solidified,
taken human forms; sinews traced
by sandworms, pebble-nipples,
eyes that refuse to recede.

They stand, seem to whisper
the sand has risen, and solidified
to dog-walkers following trails
left by sandworms. Pebbles nip

the surface with hungry bites.
They stand, seem, whisper
stories of what will happen
to dog-walkers following trails.

Until, hit by the rise, they crack under
the surface – its hungry bites
puncture their limbs. They forget
the stories of what will happen.

Just as you forget the tale made
of sandworms, pebbled-nipples,
and non-eyes that glared when
the sand had risen and solidified.

Journey

The sand is
forms; sinews traced
by
eyes that refuse to

rise

. nip

the hungry

stories of
walkers following

the crack under
the surface –
. They forge
the stories of what will happen.

forget the
worms
eyes red
sand di ed.

our

and

for sin s race

by

use

the hungry

stor es

crack under

the surf

. for

t e st s happen.

get the

worms

and di e

o r

f ace

the hung

or

the

pen

Endnotes to a History of the Sea

After Kristina Marie Darling

The terror of the still chair, the quietness of the sunbeam
cutting through the chords; the song of doors. Seas
couple with lands but a sea prefers the bloodstream
of its own kind. The tongue of the earth seizes

pebbles. Much like the human tongue, it is its strongest muscle.
Note that Noah did not consider the turtles.
The bookmark shifts in a southwest direction with each blink.
'A mare painted blue', 'a whale-road',

'a bunch of bananas soaked in skin'. When capsized, I think
the effects are sadly unlike that of a snowglobe.
That is not how you beat speech. My esteemed aphasia
is wrong about the origin of conflict. The original manuscript

has been lost for decades. When the sea is intercepted
by a body, filling your heart with salt, there is only euthanasia.

Poem in Which You Ask How You Can Tell Real Pearls from High Quality Fakes

For Lucy

Ultimately does it matter if the pearls are real or not?
The earth is a pearl, blinding and flawed,
nestled inside the mollusc of the milky way.
Do you prefer your pearls cultured in the art
of oology, or simply coated in fish scales?

Check if you must, where would I start to look
for your realness? By prodding your cheeks,
perhaps, holding your eyes against the light,
taking a sample of your speech for testing,
cataloguing evidence of feeling in your tone.

Communion

The weather's gained weight,
sags its pebbled belly against the tips
of the city's horns.

I've slumped, waiting for it to decide,
grotesque piñata, whether to burst
or rapture itself away.

The world has ended, or, at least,
most people have. I am no Avenger:
I have found wine spared

in collapsed cellars; it tastes of hills
now plucked out of reach. Grapes
have been crushed, made to sour

for my pleasure. Unwaged fingers
now mingle with the vines
while the wine runs down my throat.

Broken bottles, broken sky: red rain
heaves out of the cracked world.
I open my mouth for communion.

Bread Cthulhu

Based on #GBBO tweets

Craving the rustic?
Brush up on the bakers' backgrounds.
Learn their signature
flatbread.

Who's watching? I am a regular.
John's cake has a pink heart in every slice.
He'd make
a lovely boyfriend.

I make a mean
upside-down, but I need time to rise
at the turning-out.

Mushroom Picking

The dorm is compact and empty.
I'm road-fazed – the beds are
unlaced, but not mine.

My board shoulders the claw marks of old pins.
Theirs show cards with smiling bees and
carved colours. The scrambled deadweight of
my suitcase makes me stand lopsided.

In the corridor, girls prick their voices
from sparkly integuments. The wallpaper
is a stamped pattern on which sounds
recoil – it does not move.

Only the girls' timbres, rogue firecrackers
beeline and explode
leaving no trace at all.

The room isn't stale, just off-colour and
unmade; he's asleep in front of the TV.
His hand isn't red – not yet.

We've been hunting for mushrooms.
He knows where to uncover the best and
those that should not be touched.
The remote slips into the carpet.

I've run out of levels to tease on Diamond –
I hit a high score I can't
beat. So I've been counting aloud
the cracks that snag the walls

like encased thunder bolts.
I am surprised that they don't shatter
the unity of the façade.

Falls

It's late. Swans crisscross the lake of Reykjavík –
latte silks down your crisp claws and sinks
into an auburn mirror.

This alien, not even yours, is you
as it slips into the crevices, under
the path's skin. I catch its glint.

~

We stop for a picnic, drink
volcanic planes, magma injected
into solid rock.

The Hvítá river slips out of horizontal
and retches into a chink while its hairy smoke
continues on, baffled at the loss of a body.

Vagrant Fantasy

A version of Arthur Rimbaud's 'Ma Bohème'

I escaped! Fists punching my punctured
Pockets; my overcoat fast faded to a sketch;
I strode under that disappointed sky, ah!
The many mad loves I made!

You could peep through my sole
Trousers – in trance, I peeled rhymes as I ran.
My local was at Ursa Major; I sat on the kerb
And eavesdropped on my stars

Who burlesqued tenderly in the gods
Those warm September eves when I felt dew
Drops on my forehead, like stubborn wine;

Where, rhyming amongst the scarred shadows,
Like lyres I plucked the laces of my poached
Shoes, one foot against my heart!

Belleville

Art boils and is thrown into the gutter; oil spills
rainbows around the island of a dropped glove.
The tendons of windows are exposed, plastic
flapping over the guttural mouth. 'Hey love!

You In-glish?' The market's skeleton shines
its claws at night, but in this twilight only
songs are shred as the smile of the knife
cuts ripe pears in half. Beggars want your grin

to light on their burnt-out eyes. Rue de Belleville's
shirt is open, neon lights winking through for
Chinese joints and Turkish-Greek restaurants.
Offside are the labyrinths, darkened and grim

where minotaurs pulse from wall to wall
their rum breath like a thread suspended
above the groove of piss. You catch through
a broken bottle the glint of Avalon.

This cog of a hill cranks some more,
the eyes of Eiffel on your back until the top:
Pyrénées. There are no glaciers here, just iced
tea; the place looks less like another country.

Novella

After Rimbaud's 'Roman'

I

You can't be serious when you're twenty-one –
the evenings flare, a rolled joint behind your ear,
drunk on Wednesdays, university veteran!
You talk in your backyard of us all being queer.

The weed smells great on those June afternoons!
So sweet you could sleep through any exam;
the wind carries laughs, it's humming a tune
older than you, Johnny Wright's *Hello Vietnam*.

II

The sky is all yours, you spy it through brambles
palpitating like grass you would like to caress...
You think the answer's there to be unscrambled
if only the stars stopped changing their address.

June nights! Twenty-one! Easy to be wasted.
The cheapest wine is as good as any champagne...
You ramble on about the Bourdieu you tasted,
your lips crumple like a Communist campaign.

III

You bildungsroman through books until
you spot a leading lady perched on a stool,
with the fruit machine lights pulsing her still
face red, green and blue. You think of Kabul.

She calls you a kid when you try to explain
– as her long nails trot gamely on the board –
why you are superior to her boyfriend,
but she leaves with her glass, looking bored.

IV

You are in love: rented until August!
You are in love. She finds your poems laughable.
Your friends leave, your laundry starts to encrust
when at last, she responds to your madrigal!

That evening, you stroll out in the sun,
you order a kiss or a ginger beer;
you can't be serious when you're twenty-one
and there are summer evenings to premiere.

Telegrams

Based on a phonetic mistranslation of Pablo Neruda's 'Fábula de la sirena y los borrachos'

MESSAGE GOES HERE. BE BRIEF.
Hell is limp pork STOP Abba STOP the Savior STOP Zeus Olympics coloured-in animals STOP the distance Sue narrows END

MESSAGE GOES HERE. BE BRIEF.
Lisa stays sober STOP calm sweat STOP The almond grows itchier STOP does not attract STOP a remnant of the sea to relieve STOP The tartan apron says hello STOP All anxious at tavern STOP Irene delays swallowing END

MESSAGE GOES HERE. BE BRIEF.
The dusty copper of general debt STOP lips sweat boxes STOP Much love END

MESSAGE GOES HERE. BE BRIEF.
The poet is doing badass ball STOP What about the intro STOP Add soft reluctance STOP to get an idea of the power in Lalala END

MESSAGE GOES HERE. BE BRIEF.
I killed the mirror STOP probed a fleet of tornados STOP My name masts forward with more hate END

Suzanne Valadon Seen by Toulouse-Lautrec Seen by Me

He captured your eyes
when they were sullen. His hangover creased the paint
hairy yellow
thrown up on petrol wine.
You drank on tables that spread their freckles, the sky granulated.

When you paint
you make the canvas feel naked, it granulates
with the cold: ply it with wine.
Nicotine and gouache turn your fingers yellow.
You're the only person who undresses by adding layers. I

intrude on the café and collide with the wine
bottles that cluster by the coats. They're clasped in yellow
tags: vin du mois. Conversations stop painting.
Words, spread like granules,
are suspended. Your eyes

are missing from this painting.
Perhaps, they are hiding in the vines
of Montmartre, watching Paris yellow,
each blink smudging the granules,
dimming your I.

Rotting Anchors

An anchor on every roundabout
weighed down by corroding flowers
to remind us that the sea will rise

again, flood the supermarkets without
care for proper queues or opening hours.
The moon bathed in ketchup, trees fried

in sunflower oil, each chimney dipped
in hummus and that delicious pink stuff. We will
keep washing our floating cars for no purpose

other than it's what's in our script,
and brush our teeth with twigs and milk
to save ourselves from the worthless

rot, from the knowledge that we will
be spat out of the schedule.

Rusty Sea

The tide creaked to a halt on Tuesday. Fishermen's boats
sailed to its end and watched the drop (twenty metres).
On Wednesday, children walked to the wall: threw ropes,
pitched their hands like hooks to rouse the weevers.
Men lay ladders against the salty-hedge and dived.

Saturday, the sea turned brown, shutters clattered
closed to keep the stink out. Dead fish burst the surface,
seagulls flew so far in they forgot to return. Weeds clambered
up, tentacles piercing the plane, midges drew laced
patterns in the sky. We waited for the tide to start again.

Broken stones, boned sand, and wrinkled mud hurried
their layering. The sea solidified. Outside, the rocks rolled
in. Boulders, smoothed from the trip but pierced by a hole,
so that they seemed like an army of eyeballs, boldly
gathered by the wall of a sea that had turned to rust.

Glas

He warned me not to break
the surface of the water,
not yet.

Through the hatchings
drizzled gold rubbed
and licked the tips of rocks.
Shells nestled
in their prickly pits
– the oar splintered one –
bubbles rose as its insides disintegrated.

The wind wedged its burin deep in the current.
I was tinted yellow by an old life jacket;
her hair and scent tainted my neck.

Thirty-seven blues and greens coloured this scene;
there's no way to tell where the forest started.

Beg an Dorchenn

A palimpsest

The sky is crooked, already used.

Horses are eating between the rabbit burrows
near the blockhaus; the graffiti has sunk
in its wall like hieroglyphs, or an elegy.

I hear from the crêperie laughter catching fire,
the sandy pavement crackling like dry grass,
wrecks of words shelling from its crevice.

The fields extend like an unshaven jaw.
Surfers rest their shields on the monoliths,
nearby the Dutch have planted their tulips
like a flag. The eaten land gives itself easily
but edits what stays, and what is buried.

The Cornish Owlman

Sighted April 17, 1976, Mawnan Church

Gouache smudged & cracked
press knees against the lap
of cobbled nips and bite
your feathered lips to stop
you from crying back
for a ley-lined spine.

Mawnan, Maman, Mawnan, Maman,
why did you make me this bric-a-brac?

Frozen fricassee, you click
your shredded meat down
the track, hover between
the sheets of church and sky –
a smile is enough to shift the gaggles
that crouch to drag on red-eyed sticks.

Fest Noz

Soles tramp on the dampened land,
no one comes willingly to this mattress
of heather and gorse, but the harvested
sea tapped Morse on the chewed cliff
and requested our presence.

Perhaps it was that year's Ankou who called
for us, a bombard to a bagpipe, to raise sweaty faces
to the salt and turn ankles to granite.

We dance the kost ar c'hoad seven times
afraid to raise our ankles above the knees.
A crab cut in two doesn't halt its decay
and your long brown hair turns to white.

Fest Noz: Breton night party
Ankou: Death
Kost ar c'hoad: a type of Breton dance

Mélusine

For Mariner's Children

Sure, she looks human, but below
she is a snake wrapped around a cello.
The skin that cups her eyes is artificially scaled

with silver powder – in her hand she holds a crop to scald
the beast of wood and string. The stage is strewn with the wreckage
of a strange ship: amps, and wires teased into stands, lights blinkered, caged,

and an audience looks through an absent keyhole at the sparkle of her spittle.
When she stops, their breath expels, questions return: was she so little
a moment ago, when the room was bright with shades?

They swig their pints, let clumsiness invade
their veins once more. She's off-stage,
wrestling with her cello case.

Métro

Tongue-ticket swiped in the locked-deck;
don't tempt the pickpockets with your lactating technology.

The corridors here are crammed with haemoglobins
and posters of screaming babies creaming off the walls.

Soft tissue reassembles itself around seats and metal rods
to fit into the envelope of tunnel-shaped skin.

My pulse is stuffed in my handbag, stuck to used Kleenex.
I hear it vibrate, eight times, and then it stops.

Impression, Sunset

Blue plastic bag
caught by the shuffle of
a tourist
polyethylene cloud
gasped and chundered
over shoe
she carries on
her syncopating walk
swallowed fast
by the synthetic sag
of Camden

Outside the tube
a Pipi Longstocking bred with
a Mary Shelley experiment
with two cold bolts
sticking out of her neck
she's pushed to the wall
as she sings
covers
like gross medicine
you hope will make you feel
better

Past Simple

After the video game Braid

Flash back to that time we walked down Greek Street,
your thumb crushing the vein at my wrist to
direct me into the heart of the reek.

I was lost: pressed against the dense tattoo
of a city. From printed cobbles, fonts
screamed: "Remember your shadow," a clue

to capture as you glided me beyond
the howling windows to the lisping taps
of a pub you said you'd be keen to haunt.

~

Inside the map, I can marvel at the fact
that I've lost your arm.
The sun burns sharper when I storm
right, then back.

I can rewind to the tube stop, where it began,
make us detach,
say that – I can't stay, hope you understand.
There's a show I have to catch.

Introduction to My Love

This is an interdisciplinary thesis about the role of my love for you – how it manifests itself, and how it is employed to communicate socio-political meanings. I argue that my love drew inspiration from the theatrical stage to effectively communicate its messages. In particular, I am interested in the unofficial stages: the unpublished or unperformed stage, the stage that isn't sanctioned by the government, and the stage that spills out into the streets from the bedroom. Today is a time of creative experimentation for us thanks to the relaxation of censorship and privilege. This thesis chooses an approach that embraces our similar journeys in this field of study, and investigates the role of my love in this speech. Therefore, the methodology chosen for this thesis will be visual analysis, in which I will place my love for you within its wider historical context. In other words, I will be using thematic case studies of examples of my love with the understanding that part of their meaning derives from my love's relationship with other cultural entities, such as chocolate. This research has been peer-reviewed, and though it is limited in its scope, it demonstrates the rich potential of my love and points to a field of endeavour that I hope will inspire and promote further research in the future.

Sing Bird

<table>
<tr><td>Vile</td><td>Birds fried to the wires — electric funambulism</td></tr>
<tr><td>Violins</td><td>played by the jaded weaves of a rainstorm</td></tr>
<tr><td>Violins steal</td><td>sautéed voices trapped by melted claws</td></tr>
<tr><td>Violin-stealth</td><td>— the surprising street-corner orchestra</td></tr>
<tr><td>Violins steal the vows</td><td>of a shackled bandstand of brothers</td></tr>
<tr><td>Violins steal the voices</td><td>that have lost the page and wing-it</td></tr>
<tr><td>Violins steal the voices-off</td><td>with some gin-soaked inspiration</td></tr>
<tr><td>Violins steal the voices of whim</td><td>but I've seen how their jaws open</td></tr>
<tr><td>Violins steal the voices of women</td><td>under stress</td></tr>
<tr><td>'Violins steal the voices of we men too'</td><td>mechanically</td></tr>
<tr><td>Violins steal the voices of women to put in there</td><td>as if they had fried in their</td></tr>
<tr><td>Violins steal the voices of women to put in their</td><td>cage of shoulders and hips</td></tr>
</table>

Ruff

'A Ruffe, Is one of the strangest Fowls that is; for you shall see a hundred of them together; and not one of them like the other'
Family Magazine, 1741

Gruff unshaved pit from which erupts
a sharpened tip – Betty-punk, full
of spunk, 'specially when taking a lek.

Your fight is fluff, two wannabe
Brummells puffing at their neck cloths –
but ill-equipped without Beau's quips.

You mistrust your name – miss the thrust
of your Greco-Latin: Venus with an axe,
Ares sailing a scallop shell.

The reeves don't heave to the ground
for your muddied-regal ear-tufts – watch
the white satellites preen as you fight

and wonder, years later, what happened
to your young – those three cobalt eggs
fired with shots of ink – what was it for?

The Great Indoors

waking up next to a spider • accidentally swallowing chewing-gum in my sleep • having my eyeballs popped by a needle • being stranded alone at a bar • being thrown under a train • places where nothing is moored • places where everything is stapled • the wolf of my childhood nightmares • the crawl of a tidal wave over the horizon • not finding the light switch in the dark • becoming lactose intolerant • my life being in the hands of men who've never been poor • losing all my teeth • falling for you

Head Start

You will give birth to a serial killer, you say.
So you replenish your shelves and smash your radio.

It is time to defriend your loved ones from Facebook
and build a safe room at the back of your shower
with padded walls and a button that calls your favourite
gameshow. "Man is the warmest place to hide,"[1] he'll say
so you've amped the thermostat and walk around naked,
the bump protruding like a sweaty punch.

---

[1] *The Thing* (1982)

I Heart You

There are words on the fridge.
They're magnetic.
"I liver you, with all my lungs."
"January breaks 50% off…"
There are pictures of cats, newspaper cuttings
with words and letters blacked out.
"I stomach you, I do, but I don't brain you.
Let's skin. And glove your holes".
"Sweet, sharp, sophisticated and full…"
The fridge door has lost its suction;
the man living in it never turns the light off.
"Despot daughter a mini-dictator".
There is inside, next to the peppered cheese,
a gaudy matrioshka.
"(pictured above, dancing)"
There is on her face a black
moustache; it might as easily
be snot, or a spot.

The Night We Saw a Glow-worm

I refused to embrace the impending
building, braked, made you promise
we'd wine once still.

You took a glass, kept it empty,
we sat by torchlight on a dining set
meant for children,
let ourselves be eaten by mosquitoes.

I saw it first, a lone eye waking in the grass.
We thought it must be electrical, too bold
to be alive, a toy on standby.
Glow-worms live in packs, you pronounced.

I pressed it, felt its body melt.
I think it's a wasp, I said,
not believing myself.

Death of the Author

After The Author died His improvised foundation seized His laptop in the name of historical research. 'Just think!' enthused a spokesman, 'years of labour have been saved through this coup. Now we do not need to guess when He was working; all the data is in this stronghold'. A team of hackers worked on deciphering His passwords with relative success: 'We still can't access His Facebook account, but we suspect it includes the word 'jizzwizz.''

His student room was stripped, bills surgically reconstructed from the shredder, and photographic evidence of the contents of His fridge stored. The number of odd socks in his drawer was meticulously catalogued.

The foundation evicted the rest of His building and listed it a Grade II. No. 203 was transformed into a menagerie for the life forms found in The Author's bedsit. 'This is invaluable!' exclaimed the spokesperson, gingerly pointing to a sleepy fly. 'Now we know the source of inspiration behind His epic poem, 'Quit Bugging Me.''

His magazines were confiscated for a new government-funded PhD: 'No Sex Please, We're British: a Study on the Influence of Print Pornography on The Author's Later Work.'

Cyrano de Bergerac Takes a Last Bow

He says *fuck you* to Death, *for looking at my nose,*
raises a glass to the sky that clouds like a noose.
The moon's a limp pancake, dripping with syrup.
He pours more wine; the cork still has its stirrup.

He knows the bottom of the glass is near but beauty
is in the useless half-swig, the attempt to bounty
unbroken beads of wine on the tongue for a second
longer, to feel it slip away and still think it extant.

Yes! he cries, *You take everything away from me!*
He surveys the debris of bloodied glass, frowning.
But when I go, there's something unsmashed
I can claim's still mine, my fucking panache.

Saturday Night at La Mars

For Ariane

Dithered through four streets ditched by crowds
to the mythical place where elders drank after
school gates closed and no challenges were met.

The door was guarded by a three-bodied Cerberus
licking salt from its cheeks. Its single head swung,
while more of its bodies, captive indoors, lit the fuse

and ran behind the bar to hide from their insider
laughter, ammunition to dry stocks of Breton cider.

Erect

After the ancient Egyptian story The Tale of Two Brothers

Bata's genitals are no secret. It is written that he cut them off
in Zizzi's to prove his honesty, and then fed them to the fish.
The living wallpaper had never tasted such treats before.

Of his heart, he claimed it was encrusted in a spine.
"My heart is hidden in the thickening bark of a pine!"

But when Bata's roots were torn up, and the trunk powdered,
a splinter made its way into her mouth. A tree grew
inside her womb, the nurses had never seen such a green baby.

It groaned and creaked as the forceps
took hold of its head and heaved the body out, splintering
the mother like two halves of a shell. And so, Bata lived again.

The Fates

Morta's cut the line, shoved a granny into a display
of batteries and throwaway cameras. Decima catches
her as she falls, dislodges a shelf of tinned cassoulet.

Nona can't find the special carrier she'd stitched,
small as a marble. She's emptied her contents on the tiles.
Her pockets are mostly full of sweets glued to receipts and

black sand – tea leaves burst from their bag. From the aisle
Security asks Nona to leave, doesn't understand
that Morta's legging it out of the shop with stolen crisps.

Nona cups her treasures in her hands, watches sweets lisp
away; toddlers belly dive to catch them before they vanish.
This isn't how it used to be, moans Decima, tearing her list.

In the Garden of Death

After Hugo Simberg

pebbles ricochet against sallow phalanges,
a patella creaks at every step, flies suckle
tibias, or dart in and out of sockets.

You might mistake them for some *bêtes de scènes*
with their unretractable teeth, smiling at the plants:

myrtles, chrysanthemums, forget-me-nots,
butterflies grounded or calendulas,
flowers star-shaped, laddered or spiked...

As you join them, you'll finger your nasal
concha in hope. It's useless
to aspire to senses, you have no tongue.

Their shining skulls are the only palpable
thing amongst the painted flats: the flora
Crayola drafts they try to cup in their hands.

Good God that's a lot of shake

Buffy (Series 6, Episode 9)

It never mattered that your magic was a lopsided sketch,
all triangular girls and the maelstrom of a sun,
pinned to the fridge door and beamed at.

Only now does your lack of respect
for perspective
trouble.

No one will mind if you erase
that house and draw a rainbow in its stead:
they know your architecture came back wrong.

On this day you sprinkle
plaster over your crush
in the hope a stone will grow
upon its heart.

In unlit alleys
your skin is taut
like a bin liner;
you rip it open
and let your rat
bolt out.

Wipe the Blade Clean on the Grass

For Angela Carter

At night, the Korrigan's silkworm
hair lit up the dandelion seeds;
he made stars retract their claws.
By day, his hair was brittle white,
his eyes two eggs of dried-out blood.

Wipe the blade clean on the grass,
the hair, the eyes, must all come off.

At night, he buried his treasure under
the heaving stomach of the dolmen:
love that shined like a trout's back.
By day, the gold transformed to dust,
and cork, and skins of spiders.

Wipe the blade clean on the grass,
the heart, the lungs, must be cut off.

At night, his voice was smooth as yolk,
he sang of the moon, but not of God,
he scaled, he furred across the range.
By day, his voice muttered and squeaked,
a mouseish phlegm played hide and seek.

Wipe the blade clean on the grass,
the songs, the sounds, must be plucked off.